Young Readers

LEVEL 2

STAR WARS®

USE THE FORCE!

WRITTEN BY MICHAEL SIGLAIN

ART BY S... ...ND PILOT STUDIO

D0412475

EGMONT
We bring stories to life

First published in Great Britain 2015
by Egmont UK Limited, The Yellow Building,
1 Nicholas Road, London W11 4AN.

ISBN 978 1 4052 7782 2
60530/1
Printed in Singapore

To find more great *Star Wars* books, visit www.egmont.co.uk/starwars

Stay safe online. Any website addresses listed in this book are correct at the
time of going to print. However, Egmont is not responsible for content hosted
by third parties. Please be aware that online content can be subject to change
and websites can contain content that is unsuitable for children.
We advise that all children are supervised
when using the internet.

Luke wanted to learn the ways of the Force and become a Jedi Knight.

Luke flew his X-wing fighter
to a distant swamp planet.

Luke was looking for Yoda,
an old and wise Jedi Master.
Luke wanted Yoda to teach him
the secrets of the Force.

Luke's X-wing fighter lost power
and crashed into a giant swamp.

Luke and R2-D2 made it to shore
and met a funny little green alien.
The alien took them to his home.
The alien was Yoda!

Yoda didn't look like a strong
and mighty Jedi Master.
But he agreed to teach Luke
how to use the Force.

The Force is a special energy field that can be used for good or evil.

Luke trained with Yoda
strapped to his back.

He ran through the swamps,
swung on slimy vines,
and even stood on his hands.

Then Luke saw a strange cave. It was scary and cold and filled with the dark side of the Force.

Luke took his weapons and
slowly ventured into the cave.

Luke was shocked to see
Darth Vader inside the cave!

Luke fought him and failed.
Then Darth Vader vanished.
He wasn't really there at all.
It had been a test from Yoda.

Luke still had much to learn,
so he kept training.

But there was trouble in the swamp.
R2-D2 beeped and whistled to Luke.
The X-wing sank into the swamp.
Luke didn't know how to get it out.

Then Yoda spoke to Luke.
He told him to use the Force.
"Do. Or do not," Yoda said.
"There is no try."

Luke used the Force, and
the X-wing began to rise.

Luke could not get the
ship out of the swamp.

It sank deeper into the water.
Luke could not raise the X-wing.
He gave up and walked away.

Yoda used the Force.
He raised the ship out
of the water.

Yoda really was strong in the Force!
Luke could not believe it.

That was why he had failed.
He did not believe in himself.
He did not believe in the Force.

Luke trained even harder.
He listened to Yoda and
practised day and night.

He learned how to use the Force.
He could even move things
with his mind!

While using the Force,
Luke saw a vision of the future.

His friends were in trouble.
Darth Vader had captured them.
Luke knew that it was a trap,
but he still had to save them.

Luke decided to leave
the swamp planet.
He said goodbye to Yoda
and promised to return.

Then he flew away in his X-wing.

Luke was ready to use the Force. He would save his friends and become the greatest Jedi of all!